Gamblers

Gamblers

The tested and tried life
of a pastor Vs.
Jack the little devil &
Jack the reckless gambler

P. Dalton Simms

XULON PRESS

Xulon Press
2301 Lucien Way #415
Maitland, FL 32751
407.339.4217
www.xulonpress.com

© 2022 by P. Dalton Simms

All rights reserved solely by the author. The author guarantees all contents are original and do not infringe upon the legal rights of any other person or work. No part of this book may be reproduced in any form without the permission of the author.

Due to the changing nature of the Internet, if there are any web addresses, links, or URLs included in this manuscript, these may have been altered and may no longer be accessible. The views and opinions shared in this book belong solely to the author and do not necessarily reflect those of the publisher. The publisher therefore disclaims responsibility for the views or opinions expressed within the work.

Unless otherwise indicated, Scripture quotations taken from the King James Version (KJV) – *public domain*.

Paperback ISBN-13: 978-1-6628-4861-2
Ebook ISBN-13: 978-1-6628-5115-5

Acknowledgment

On the eighth of August 2019 P. Dalton Simms the sole author and writer of the children book A Boy Named Jesus, once again, have decided to write a second book titled:

Gamblers
The Tested and Tried Life of a Pastor
VS.
Jack the Little Devil &
Jack the Reckless Gambler

I humbly give thanks to the Holy Spirit who is truly the source of knowledge and inspiration, which guided both my fingers and my thoughts throughout the entire writing of this book.

This book can relate to stories of real-life events or even fictional characters.

People I believe, can identify with stories in their past or present lives, found in this book, especially people of faith. I do hope and pray that life challenges may result in happy conclusions.

To God Almighty always is the glory.

Chapter One

Pastor Titus Daniel was the fourth in line to become a pastor in the Daniel's family. He was known to be a very honest, kind, and respectable man. All who had the privilege of meeting or knowing him had no problem in agreeing what a wonderful human-being he was.

Most, if not all the people in his congregation, said he is an anointed man of God. it is no wonder considering his background.

First to comment, he was practically born and raised up in the church, constantly hearing and seeing his father and grandfathers preaching, teaching, and ministering to people, through his youthful years. On that note one could agree to his godly image and vast knowledge of God.

Pastor T.D, as he was affectionately known, had already fathered three children, all of which were girls, including a set of twins and one miscarriage also, a girl child. Once again, for the fifth time, his wife, Audrey Daniels, gave birth to another girl child.

As much as they both trusted and had faith in God, Pastor Daniel was a bit worried that this might lead to a monumental change in him not having a son to continue his lineage as a pastor as did his past three generations.

However, he and his wife constantly prayed, hoping, and trusting in the Lord who gives children. Years went by, and still no son was born to the Daniel family, yet still, faith is the victory that can overcome all past, present, and future challenges.

Then as faith would allow, on a very stormy day, a very strange thing happened. There was a knock at the door of the Daniel's house. Audrey Daniel opened the door and saw Sean Patrick, the son of

Tatiana, who is a faithful woman of God and a member of the church that Pastor Daniel pastored.

Come rain or come shine, Tatiana would go to the church even if no other person showed up, she would make it her point of duty to go there and make sure that the house of God was in order.

And because of that action. she acquired the name "Mother in Zion"

Audrey Daniel said to the young man, "Hi, Sean Patrick, what brings you to my home in such severe weather? I hope all is well."

She then beckoned him to come inside and took the young man's rain cloak and his hat then offered him a seat and a mug of hot cocoa.

He politely thanked her, then asked her if Pastor Daniel was at home. He said that he has a message for him from his mother, Tatiana

Pastor Daniel was in his study. His wife called out to him, Titus, "Can you please come to the sitting room? You have a visitor."

Soon as Pastor Daniel saw Sean Patrick, he got a bit worried. However, he greeted him and told him to follow him to his study.

Pastor Daniel said, "Let us pray." Dear Lord, we thank you for being so faithful and for guiding this young man safely to our home in this severe weather'

Pastor Daniel said, "Now Sean Patrick, is everyone ok? Yes, Pastor, everyone is ok, my sisters Naomi and Makayla together with my brothers, Michael and Andrew all went with our dad to see his mom So, my parents both agreed that my younger sisters, Emilia, and Symira stay back at home with my mom and I."

Pastor Daniel patted Sean Patrick on his shoulder and said he was proud of him, in hearing that his father had such confidence in him.

The boy continued by saying, "My mother was worried as to whether the church was ok since tomorrow is the day of worship, and Pastor, you know my mother. No weather can hardly keep her away from making the house of God ready for worship."

Pastor Daniel smiled and said, "He already knows. May the good Lord continue to bless and keep her and her family safe." Sean Patrick said, "Amen.

Chapter One

However as soon as my mother returned home, she asked me to hurry to your place and ask you to come see her. Fortunately for us, we all live in proximity of each other's home"

Pastor Daniel Kissed his wife and told her that he was about to go over to Tatiana's house to find out why she sent for him. His wife Audrey said, "Please, be careful out there you both, I will be praying for you."

Chapter Two

When Pastor Daniel and the boy arrived at the boy's home, they were dripping wet. Tatiana greeted them, took their wet clothes, and gave them towels to dry off.

Then she asked her son Sean Patrick to go watch his younger sisters Emilia and Symira while Pastor Daniel and her had a talk

At first, she seemed reluctant, not knowing where to begin, until Pastor Daniel held her hands and prayed.

"Lord and Creator of the universe, please remove every anxiety and fear from Tatiana. I am quite sure, Lord, that You already know the reason she sent for me. Please, grant her the courage to speak what is on her mind. Thank you, Lord.

Tatiana told Pastor Daniel that she went to the church to make sure the place was in a suitable condition for worship service, upon entering, she noticed an object on the top stairs of the church.

There was also a cry coming from whatever it was. She realized it was the cry of a child.

So, without any hesitation, she went to check and there in a basket covered with a blanket was a baby.

She removed the blanket and the sweetest little face smiled upon seeing her, she then looked around to see if there was anyone else, she called out, but no one responded.

She picked up the basket, removed the baby, and there was a note which read: "Dear Pastor Daniel, this is my sweet baby boy Jackson, I have weighed all my options. I absolutely love my son, but I am unable to care for him anymore. And I am afraid of what might transpire if frustration takes over and I might hurt myself or my innocent child.

Pastor Daniel, I have heard wonderful things about you, that you are a good person who serves the Lord with reverence.

And that both you and your wife have only daughters, so please take my son as your own and raise him up in the fear of God.

My only request is that you allow him to keep the name I gave him at birth which is Jackson/aka jack for short he is now three months and five days old.

Jackson cries when he is hungry, and that is because I hardly have the food to feed him as a child should be fed.

I have not heard from the man who fathered him even before his birth. As he treated me so badly, I ran away living on the street for months. So please, I beg of you, take my son as your very own. I will be hoping and praying that one day he might become someone as noble as you are.

With tearful eyes and a sad heart, I truly regret doing this, I will visit in spirit and in thoughts. I have not disclosed my name in the note as I would like to remain anonymous. Goodbye for now and may God bless you and all that you hold dear to your heart. Signed, a sad but hopeful mother of one precious child goodbye my son. I love you.

Chapter Three

Tatiana had tears in her eyes but joy in her heart as Pastor Daniels took the note and read its contents.

Tatiana was also sure that it was God who sent her to the church so that she could find the basket with the baby, and God had answered Pastor Daniels's long awaiting prayers in having a son of their own, hoping that by faith and God's intervention, his son would also become a pastor, a great man of God, so as his past generations.

Pastor Daniels was a bit concerned as this was a tricky situation which could and should involve the law. Also, if this is of God, he would have to go in fasting and praying, in seeking answers from God.

So, to Tatiana, he said, "Can we sleep on this until tomorrow? By then hopefully I might have answers for you, but first, let me go home and break this news to my wife.

We will come by tomorrow so that we can take the child to the authority and report the matter.

Do you think you will be able to keep the child until tomorrow, since you are the one that found him? Plus, the weather is so bad I do not want to risk taking him outside.

Tatiana said yes Pastor T.D.

They prayed and said goodbye. When Pastor Daniel got home, his wife and children were waiting up for him, pacing the floor and wanting to know in detail why Tatiana asked him to come over to her house in such severe weather.

However, he was too exhausted, and more like confused to explain anything, so he told them goodnight, "See you all in the morning. Let me rest and compose myself, then I will be able to tell it all.

But, for the record, I believe, or I hope by faith, God might have answered another one of our prayers." With that been said, his wife and children became even more curious.

Ms. Daniels did not allow her husband to sleep and cheat her out of hearing what had transpired over at Tatiana's house. "Pastor Daniel smiled as he sat up in bed and told his wife all about what he had encountered earlier. How Tatiana had gone to the church as usual, bless her heart and effort.

She had shown to him the most precious baby boy, and it seemed as if someone had placed the child inside a basket and left it on the steps of the church with a note requesting that he, Pastor Daniels, take the child as his own and raise him up."

"It is a boy!" exclaimed his wife, "Tell me more."

Pastor Daniel said, "Calm down, my dear wife. Please, do not get your hope up too soon."

She replied, "Don't you recall the Bible story of the baby Moses? How his mother placed him in a basket, and set it on the river Nile in Egypt, to save him from those evil ones who were destroying the Hebrew's boy babies?"

He then said he did not want to say this in the presence of the children, as he did not want it going any further until he was certain. His wife agreed. They prayed, hugged, and said goodnight.

Ms. Daniels could not sleep that night. Instead, she prayed and worshiped God, silently thanking him for answering their prayers and sending them a son, even by the means of adoption.

Pastor Daniel woke up the next morning and found his wife knitting a baby blue blanket and humming hymns. He said to her, "Don't start counting your blessings in this matter too fast," but she just kept on humming and knitting.

Chapter Four

The phone rang, and it was Tatiana, mother in Zion, with report on baby Jacksons throughout the night. She said Jackson slept very well and that her children were asking all kind of questions about the baby and were fussing over him.

However, she did not let off too much information, instead, she told them that he was visiting. "It's a boy, and his name is Jackson, Aka 'Jack' for short," she laughed and said they did not want to go to school, instead they begged to stay home and help to care for baby Jackson.

But she managed to change all of that by, promising that by God's will, they would see more of him.

Tatiana asked Pastor Daniel what time she should expect him? and how did his wife Audrey, responded to the news about baby Jackson

He said, "That is a long story. Let us save that one for later. See you in an hour, God willing, bye for now, and remember to keep on praying. Say hi to little Jackson for us."

Audrey Daniel reminded him that his great grandfather was nick named "Pappy Jackson." he smiled as he pondered these things in his heart.

Pastor Daniel, together with Audrey, went to see Tatiana. When Audrey Daniel saw baby Jackson and he smiled at her, it was love at first sight.

Pastor Daniel was worried for her because if it did not work out in favor of them adopting the child, his wife might be disappointed. However, he would trust by faith.

It was such an intense moment as they approached the police station to make the report. Tatiana told her story about finding baby Jackson.

Jackson slept through the whole episode, not having a clue as to what his future would be or where or with whom he might end up.

Unfortunately for them, little Jackson had to be handed over to child protective services until future investigation, which made them all incredibly sad, anyhow it was all a process, after the case goes before the court, there will be a hearing in which the court would give its ruling. Then they will be notified..

They got into the pastor's car, prayed for journey mercy, and asked God to please watch over baby Jackson and his mother, hoping God would bring him back safely to them.

After the prayer, no one said another word until Pastor Daniel dropped Tatiana off at her home and they said their goodbye.

Pastor Daniel went to his study to pray and started preparing his sermon for the next day worshipped he named it, "When God Says 'Yes,' He Means 'Yes,' and Can No One Say 'No.'"

He had taken pictures of baby Jackson, so he took out his phone and started looking at them he called his wife to come and see them, and to discuss the matter between them both, the possibilities of adoption, if the court gave custody of baby Jackson over to them, as the note found with the baby requested.

After that no one made any mention on the matter. Instead, their lives continued as usual.

Chapter Five

Tatiana's husband returned home from his trip to see his mother; Tatiana told him of the strange encounter she had in finding baby Jackson. He suggested that she do not get too involved in matters of such sorts. As he was not prepared to have his family name splashed over the news for the kidnapping of a child. He said he already had enough problems of his own.

Tatiana disagreed. She said she believed that it was a miracle from above and that the child deserves a home with a good family, and the Daniels were the right choice Her husband said he hoped that everything worked out well for everyone involved.

Weeks went by, and no one from Child Protective Services contacted the Daniels however, they kept hoping and praying that any day now someone would.

Ms. Daniels was the one most certain that baby Jackson was theirs, and so she was sure that he would come back to them very soon—by faith, she believed.

Early the next day, the phone rang. The person identified herself as miss Debora Sutton a social worker from child protective services, she further stated that the Daniels should come to the department for questions concerning baby Jackson.

They got an appointment for the very next day. The Daniel's asked if the baby was ok, and will they be able to see him?

The social worker replied by saying she was not able to answer any of their questions and that they should just save all questions until they came to the department.

However, if they were not able to keep the appointment, they had no obligations to do so, but upon hearing that, they quickly said on the contrary, "We both definitely will be there, God willing," and that it was more than a pleasure for them to hear from the department.

They said thanks and goodbye, the phone hung up.

They were so elated that they called Tatiana and told her that they had gotten appointment at the children protective service department to discuss matters concerning baby Jackson.

Tatiana let out a sigh of relieve and started singing praises to the God of Heaven and earth, she even said that it would be a pleasure to accompany them, except that her husband was not too thrilled with her getting involved in such smatter. However, he wished them all the best in getting the baby boy.

It was a long night filled with suspense; the Daniels hardly slept that night.

Early the next morning, they dropped off the girls at school and the youngest at Tatiana's house. Praying, they headed down to the children department. When they got there, they went straight to the receptionist desk and asked to see miss Deborah Sutton, they sat and waited. Finally, after waiting in suspense, a woman came to them. She politely greeted them and directed them to her office.

After asking them questions, she stated that the child was in the hospital. Pastor Daniel asked, "Why, what happened?" She stated that it seemed as if the child was malnourished, and to make matters worse, rear drugs in his blood."

"Oh no!" exclaimed Ms. Daniel. "Poor baby, will he be, ok?"

Pastor Daniel said to his her, "Do not worry my dear. We will pray that the Lord will make him well."

Ms. Sutton explained that they had published an ad for anyone knowing the whereabouts of the child's biological parents, stating they should come forward within a period not exceeding eight to six weeks. After that, the child can be adoption.

Chapter Five

She said that it had now been over two months, and there had been no response.

The matter was now handed over to the court for reviews.

However, if they were sure, and ready to assume responsibilities in adopting the child, it would be a process. They said, "Yes, without a doubt. We, the Daniels, are sure and ready to proceed. They read and sign documents, agreeing to the terms and conditions,

The phone rang to inform that baby Jackson was fine and ready to be release from the hospital.

Big wow! On that note, All praises to Almighty God.

However, they had to leave, because they had to pick the girls up from school, fortunately for them, very soon they would get a chance to have supervised visits with baby Jackson so that the baby Jackson and the Daniel's family can get acquainted.

Not to mention that temporary visits can help the court to decide on granting the adoption of baby Jackson to the Daniels

Or the Daniels too can be sure in deciding on adopting baby Jackson or not.

Chapter Six

Finally, they received a letter from the department allowing them supervised visits with a social worker assigned to the case concerning baby Jackson, after supervised visits, the court ruled in favor of the Daniels.

So, baby Jackson became Jackson David Daniel. Celebration followed right after the Christening took place, by none other than Pastor Daniel pronouncing blessings on his adopted son Jackson David Daniel.

Jackson got so much love and care, spoiled rotten by his four sisters, and members of the church's congregation. Jackson was a handsomely fine and cute baby.

Crying and fussy at times, yes, but this was quite normal and expected as he became adjusted to his new family and surroundings.

Most nights they hardly got any sleep, if not for the Daniel's taking turns in feeding, cuddling, and diaper changing baby Jackson.

Talk about pacifying, baby Jackson refused to use a pacifier, he even refused to sleep in his crib Ms. Daniel suggested to her husband that Jacksons crib be into their bedroom, as Jackson may have been sleeping with his mom who might not have had proper accommodations for them both.

Things only got worse as the days, months, went by. Jackson would throw tantrums, bite, and scratch, he would throw his food and drink.

Yet still all the Daniels did was love him, prayed, and hope that their adopted son would someday change into a humble and obedient child.

The twin girls were not so accepting of baby Jack anymore, they even asked their parents to send him packing, but their parents said that they would not send them packing no matter what they did and so as Jackson.

Whenever the family went on vacation, Jackson made it so unpleasant for everyone.

He would yell and scream so loudly, that Pastor Daniel had to stop the car pull over on the service road or a rest area hoping that Jackson would calm down, Jackson would remove his diaper with urine or poop and toss it anywhere. Raising Jackson was not an easy job plus Audrey Daniel had another young child just under one year old and adopting Jackson with a toddler and three other children was more than a handful.

If not for Tatiana stopping by at times to give a helping hand, things might have become unbearable, bless her heart.

Lest anyone might forget, it was Tatiana who played a big part in them getting baby Jackson. Surprisingly now, she was one showing less tolerance for him, she even mentions that he seemed a little devilish.

Years had passed, and Jackson attended Pre-K, at Saint Benedict of Mercy. It was a religious setting, but after the first week at Saint Benedict of Mercy, Jackson acquired the name "Jack the little devil."

The school told the Daniel's his adopted parents not to bring him back the following week, as Jackson was uncontrollable.

They were very embarrassed, but still, they loved and cared for him as all their four other children.

The Daniels home schooled Jackson until age four, which was extremely hard. He was a difficult, tyrannical little boy. One had to think it over even if taking him outside.

Going to the supermarket was the only treat, as Jackson liked riding inside the shopping cart and eating his good boy treats. It was only the day before that Jackson had thrown his good boy treat, an ice cream cone, at a lady who was also shopping at the same mall, and he giggled. The woman yelled at Jack and said to Jack's adopted mother, "control or keep your little devil at home."

Chapter Six

Ms. Daniel quickly apologized to the lady and said, "He is just a small boy not a little devil."

The lady replied by saying, "In your eyes, he is a small boy, but I can see a little devil in him."

Audrey's eyes filled up with tears, not accepting that her precious child was anything comparing to a little devil, he is just a little baby boy.

She called her husband crying and told him what had happened at the mall. He told her to come straight to the church, as he was there preparing a sermon.

There, he consoled her, they prayed about it and played a while with Jackson. Then left to get the girls at school, and they all went to the park, had ice cream, fed the ducks at the lake, and went home.

Ms. Daniel's was bothered because of what the woman said to Jackson at the mall, but she trusted by faith and with time, Jackson would turn out to be an upstanding human being.

She knew that God was able to do far beyond what no human could do. So, she would just keep on loving and caring for her God-given adopted son Jackson.

Chapter Seven

Now it was time for Jackson to start kinder garden and the fear of him not accepted crept into the mind of the Daniels, however surely, fear was not of God, so that night, they prayed and left it all in the hands of God.

Surprisingly, the next morning, Jackson was not in his bed, or anywhere in the house.

They called out his name but no answer. "What in the world is the meaning of this said Pastor Daniel?"

Pastor Daniel checked the front door It, locked, so he checked the back door, and it opened. Ms. Daniel was down in the basement, looking and calling out Jack's name while the girls looked under the beds, couches, cupboards, and wherever possible, until they heard Pastor Daniels calling them to come and to see that the back door was open and there were track marks of little feet leading to the woods. They followed it for a while, calling out for Jack but with no trace, sound, clues, or any signs from Jack.

Then the girls begun to cry for their little brother Jack. "Where could he have gone off to? Did someone enter the home and take him away?" But no because there were no signs of any other foot marks.

So, they walk back to the house, tired, worried, and sad, wondering what had really happened to little Jack. Once again, they searched the entire house, and the girls refused to even go to school because Jack was missing.

They all sat down comforting each other and tried to compose themselves.

"Jack, where are you?" Finally, Ms. Daniel said, "We should report it to the authorities, but first let us call Tatiana and her husband Ronald to hear if they have any suggestions."

Tatiana and her husband told the Daniels to try and calm down as they will drop their children off at school and come by as soon as possible.

When they arrived, it was a moment of grief. They prayed, and discussed the matter among themselves, and came to a decision of reporting the incident to the authorities' who then said it would not be classified as a missing person for seventy-two hours.

However, the authorities will put out an alarm, considering it is about a child They should go home and report back if there were any news on the child, the authorities also would contact them if any reports came in of such concerning a child.

So, they headed back to the Daniels' home, and to their surprise, when they got home, Jack was sitting on the front port, talk about happy.

No one did not even bother to ask jack any questions or scolded him. Instead, they just picked him up, went inside, and checked his person to see if any mark or marks were on him, Jack seemed simply fine, a bit exhausted yes, sleepy, thirsty, and hungry. Ms. Daniel took Jack inside and gave him a bath, something to eat, and a cool glass of milk, plus lots of hugs and kisses from everyone.

They called the authorities to report that Jackson was safe and back home.

Jack fell asleep, but before he did, he kept mumbling something sounding like he was saying, "The cat, the cat."

Them, it dawned on them that they did not see Bobcat, all morning, also Pastor Daniel recalled that he had opened the back door and the Bobcat went outside, so he had left it open so that Bobcat could get back inside.

In assumption to that, Pastor Daniel said that Jack must have gotten up and saw the cat outside and because the door was open,

Chapter Seven

he went out to the cat, Bob the cat had a way of taking off into the woods not wanting to come inside, so Jack must have gone after it and lost his way back home, just maybe that solved the puzzle Three days had passed, and still, Bobcat had not returned home, nothing unusual for Bobcat.

As he would leave for days until Ms. Daniel cooked meatballs. Bob the cat could smell it from wherever he was and would defiantly show up. unfortunately, this time, Bobcat still had not returned.

Chapter Eight

"Jackson Daniel," said teacher Marquise. "Can you please sit and stop disturbing the class?" But Jackson just threw himself on the floor and started to scream, which caused other children to follow.

This was a pattern of Jackson Daniel. The teacher had to call a recess and reported the incident to the principal that Jackson was so uncontrollable, and he even stated that if Jackson had to continue in his classroom, he would quit teaching, he even branded Jackson a sure devilish child.

Now for the third consecutive time, Jackson was known to be a little devil, this was very troubling for the Daniels family. In the space of less than five years of Jackson's life, he carried around a bad reputation.

Now in space of just three months, Jackson had been in three different kindergartens. Also, let the record show that Jackson was removed from PreK.

Sigh! "Not again," said the Daniels. Time for diagnosis, the Daniel's made an appointment for Jackson to see a medical doctor, who after evaluating him, stated that Jackson might need future evaluation and recommended counseling for the family.

Medication was prescribed for Jackson as a trial hopefully to calm him down, until future tests.

Pastor Daniel's church was losing members on account of Jackson's unbelievably bad behaviors, babies were kept away from Jackson. And as for toddlers and small children, Jackson would bite, scratch, hit, or push them to the floor. Service after service, the worst incident was when Jackson pulled out a lock of hair from a three-year-old girl's head bit and scratched her face.

Her parents got terribly upset, and the child's father called Jackson "a little devil from the pit of hell."

Some people even refused to attend that church with Jackson there. Poor Pastor Daniel he stayed on his knees for the church, his family and for Jackson to be normal. But sadly things only got worse. And on church days, Jackson has supervision.

Oftentimes, the social worker would show up to check in. Right there in eyes of the social worker, Jackson would misbehave. Anyone could infer that Jackson was a little tyrant. Just maybe that is what the worker was thinking in her mind.

Jackson was now ten years old when Ms. Daniel had to rush to her youngest daughter Breanna's room after hearing her scream, she found Jackson with his adopted sister pinned down on the bed practically lying on top of her.

She quickly pulled him off her, and for the first time, she slapped him, but Jackson charged at her and referred to her as stupid.

He grabbed her by the legs and bit her, she managed to push him out of the room and shut the door.

The little girl was so frightened and was crying, her mom hugged her and tried to console her, but she kept on saying, "Bad, bad, Jack is very bad," she "don't want to play with him anymore."

When Ms. Daniel recovered from the shock and was glad that she was at home, she wiped her daughter's tears and went to the bathroom, she applied dressing to her legs.

She then went downstairs to find that Jackson had smashed the television set, broke up other items, tossed pillow cushions on the floor, and was not in the house. She looked outside and saw Jackson riding off on his bicycle.

Poor Jackson was confused; he was a hot mess, a rebel with a cause, which no one seemed to know or even understood.

Chapter Eight

Pastor Daniel arrived home after his wife had called him to say that there was a crisis at home and that he should come home immediately.

Something needed serious attention, she had asked him to pick the girls up from school and drop them by Tatiana's until they sort this problem out.

When Pastor Daniel arrived home, she told him what she encountered earlier, but was not sure what was Jacksons intention toward his little adopted sister, considering the position he had her in.

Audrey said she was not sure if they were wrestling over something or what because neither of them said anything. The little girl just said, "Jack is bad," and Jack was not home to clarify for himself what had happened.

Pastor Daniel said to his wife, "We should be careful of what we pray for." She too said, "She has started to wonder if someone placed a curse on Jack by referring to him as a 'little devil.'"

The pastor just sighed and hoped that Jack was ok, then he went to check on his baby girl, who was hugging a teddy bear and was crying.

When she heard her dad come into the room and called her name, she got up jumped and hugged him tightly.

He kissed her cheeks, and apologized for Jack, then asked her what happened between her and Jack? She said it was over a silly one dollar.

She had saved up a dollar, and Jack wanted to borrow it to add to his three dollars he wants to buy a necktie for his father's birthday. But She said no because she also wanted to buy a gift for her father's birthday.

Tears filled up in Pastor Daniels eyes. He dropped to his knees and started sobbing, begging God to forgive him for saying, "Be careful of what you pray for."

The little girl kept crying and saying, "Sorry, Daddy, sorry." Just then, Ms. Daniel came into the room and saw her husband sobbing and asking God to forgive them for assuming the worse of Jack when his intensions were purely good.

He then explained the whole thing to her. She was so shocked because even she herself did not remember her husband's birthday.

Poor Jack, where could he be? She had slapped him and called him a tyrant in her mind and even wondered if a spell was placed on him, after been called a little devil by those people. Or did that thought come from the fact that he was not their biological child? She was so sorry, that she broke down and cried so hard that she threw up.

Jackson came home but did not go inside as he saw his adopted dad's car in the garage. He sensed trouble, so he went to his tree house in the woods.

As it got dark, they began to worry, Pastor Daniel decided to go look for his beloved son. He had a feeling as to where Jackson might be, so he took a flashlight and went toward the woods where he had helped Jackson to build a tree house. As he got close enough, he softly said, "Son," and again he said, "Son."

That voice did not sound like someone upset, so Jack answered, "Yes, Dad?" and said he wanted to stay in the tree house.

His dad said, "Ok, son. But first, can you come down for a bit so that we can talk?"

Jackson said, "What for? Do you want to also slap me"? Go away. Everyone already thinks and calls me a 'little devil,' so, Dad, now it is your turn."

But his dad said, "Oh no, son. Never have I ever cherished such a thought. Stay put. I can come up, it that ok?" Jackson did not answer, so his dad took it as a "yes" and went up into the tree house.

He said, "Hi! Son, everyone is so worried about you, even Breanna, your little sister. She even asked me to keep this one dollar and give it to you when you get home."

Jackson did not respond. His dad said, "May I sit?" Jackson nodded his head and pointed to a seat. His dad said, "Thanks, son. Can we just hold hands and pray a little while?" Jackson looked at him as if to say, "The good that will do for a little devil as me."

Chapter Eight

But his dad took his hand and prayed. He said, "Dear Lord, you gave us five girls, four are alive, and one never made it.

After the first one came, every time Audrey was with child, we hoped for a boy, but God, in Your infinite knowledge you gave us only girl children. But then it was as if Heaven smiled on us and sent us a son, our little angel Jackson. Lord, others might see him as 'a little devil,' but it does not matter what others say or think. We love him so very much.

We just want to thank You for our sweet son, Jackson, who we love so very much and would not exchange him for all the treasures in the world.

Thank you, Lord.

Jack was amazed! He jumped up and hugged his dad. He cried and said he was sorry for being such an annoying boy, but from now on, he was going to try hard to be a good.

His dad said, "Amen," hugged him, took his hand, and said, "Let us go home to a new beginning."

Chapter Nine

Years passed, Jackson did well in school. He sang on the church choir, and helped his dad to put sermons together, sometimes he even said the opening prayer and read scriptures.

All who knew the old Jackson could hardly believe what their eyes were seeing or their ears hearing—is that really Jackson Daniel? God must have touched him, and commended the Daniels for being so kind and patient with him. God bless them and their efforts.

Finally, the church was now at rest, and former members started coming back, just to see for themselves if the rumors that were all over the town were true.

Jackson was now sixteen, he finished and graduated high school as valedictorian. He gave an amazing speech at graduation, which he wrote all on his own.

There were such big applauses. His adopted parents and all who knew him were so proud of him, including his four adopted sisters who cheered on.

Then as faith would have it, the very next day, there was a loud knock at the front door of the Daniel's home.

Pastor Daniel opened the door and saw a rugged looking man in about his late thirties. He was holding a female by the lock of her hair. Pastor Daniel said, "Hello, can I ask who are you? How Can I assist you?"

But the man just shouted, "Give me my ——son!" Pastor Daniel said, "Your son? I do not understand."

The man replied while still holding the woman by her hair, "Cut the bull crap, and don't pretend as if you don't know what I am talking about." "Ok, let me formally introduce myself I am Jackson Simmons/ aka Jack the Reckless Gambler.

While I was away in prison this stupid idiot gave my son away without my consent. Now I am back on the street, and I have come to get him, so tell me, where is he?"

The woman seemed so afraid of that beast of a man. She just kept crying and saying, "Sorry," to the pastor.

The man pushed her to the ground and put his foot on her. Pastor Daniel tried to stop him, but the man punched him and pulled out a gun.

Jackson was standing by the window when he saw the man that looked such resemblance to himself, pointing a gun at his father Pastor Daniel's head and screaming at the top of his lungs, "Give me my—-son or tell me where he is before I do something I might not regret. I am ready to go back to prison for my—-son."

Pastor Daniel said, "Let us pray," which got the man even more furious. He stomped the woman some more, that she screamed in pain, but she kept saying, "Stay away from my son, you are a crazy son of a retch Go crawl back into your alligator lair!" But he kicked her even harder.

Jackson was confused, his adopted mother was down in the basement doing laundry. Jackson ran to inform her of what was transpiring outside, she told him to wait inside in case he had to call the police, she went upstairs. But soon as she opened the door and saw the gun, she fainted.

Jackson saw this, and he called for the police in no time the sirens started wailing.

The man took off and threw the gun into the wooded area. The police officers gave chase and caught up with him. The man struggled with the police officers, but they managed to restrain him and place cuffs, the police officers then investigated the matter.

The woman shouted, "He has a gun! Be careful, he has a gun!"

The police officers searched and found the gun, but it was fake, lucky for the strange man. Pastor Daniel then helped his wife to her

Chapter Nine

feet; she then got an icepack for her husband's face where the strange man had hit him.

The police officers took a statement, after hearing the full story, they advised that they take it up with the children service department in charge of such matters.

The police officers arrested the strange man and called for an ambulance to assist the abused woman who pressed charge on her abuser.

After things calmed down, Jackson had question as to who the strange, man was.

A man that was claiming back his son ... to whom was he making references? This was a day in the Daniels' lives. If ever there were problems, those were minor ones in comparison to this one.

Just the thought of them losing their only son Jackson to this obnoxious and extremely unpleasant kind of person, claiming to be Jackson's biological father, just brought on disgust, great fear, and tension.

And frankly speaking, Jackson seemed a remarkable resemblance of that strange, awful man both in image and personality. This could add up as to Jackson's past behavior while growing up, the way he functioned as a child and conducted himself, especially toward others.

Could it be that Jackson was a carbon copy of this awful man claiming to be his father? No, no, it is not true. Please, Lord, help us make this thing disappear. Let it not be a reality but a bad dream, pleaded the Daniels.

Jackson Daniel was just standing there as if frozen, wanting answers. Tears filled up in the eyes of his adopted parents. worst of all the burning thoughts of them not telling Jackson that he was adopted. Jackson asked, "Can someone please explain to me what just happened?

Who were those two people? And who is their son?

The man said his name is Jackson. My name is Jackson. The woman kept saying leave her son alone. Mom, Dad, am I adopted? Please, say something. "Jackson started yelling! As if changing back into his old image.

The Daniels were dumb struck.

"Calm down, Jackson," Pastor Daniel finally spoke. "Calm down, son. Please sit down, I will explain, but first, let us pray about this."

"There you go again, Dad, Jackson yelled, if that is who you really are. Always saying, 'Let us pray.' Can you please explain without putting God into this as if you want God to speak for you?

Ok, Dad, let me ask mom if that is who she really is. Go ahead, Ms. Daniel, explain, or will you also have to first pray?

As a matter of a fact, forget it all. I will just go down to the police station and ask to see Jackson Simmons and ask him to explain to me what this is all about.

And for the record, you both reminds me of the bible story Ananias and his wife Sap-phi-ra, how they connived, and guilt killed them both. If only they could have told the truth." He left off, slamming the door behind him, saying, "Fake Pastor and his conniving wife Audrey."

Jackson stepped outside, who was there but the woman that was with the strange tyrant of a man. Jackson looked at her and asked. "Who are you?"

She softly said, "My son, please find a place inside of your heart to forgive me. I am so sorry for the choice I made, but it was for your own good. I was in a bad place at that time in my life.

I was a hot mess, no money, no home, no father to help me with a baby. I was a rebellious teenager, I ran away from home, and got involved with your father. Soon after I got pregnant.

Them I found out from his friend Curly joe, that he was in prison for hitting a man who fell hit his head and subsequently died from his wound.

Young Jackson just stood there, staring, listening to her. "May I call you Jackson she asked? Is that your name? Because when I left you at the church, I had written a note asking Pastor Daniel to take you and raise you as his own son, and that he allow you to keep the name Jackson, Jack for short. That also is your biological father's name.

Chapter Nine

I do understand that this is a whole lot for you to take on so suddenly, however, it cannot be changed it's already done, only please give it time.

Your adopted parents, I am sure, love and care for you very much. We your biological parents also love you.

Please, do not hold this against us, I beg of you." "Your father always spoke to you in my stomach, he would say things like, 'What are you doing inside there? Jackson, my boy, is the light turned on?'" Which made Jackson smile.

She said her name was Millicent She was now thirty-two years old, and she is a registered nurse, married to Mark Hines a banker and they have four children.

She asked Jackson to take a walk with her. Jackson thought for a moment, then he went with her. They walked and talked. Jackson wanted to know why she never came to see him. She told him that she did, she even attended services at the church so that she could see him, and sometimes at the park to observe him play with his adopted sisters.

She was there that day at the church when he pulled out a lock of hair from a little girl's head bit and scratched her. She said she ran from the church, crying in fear that he was acting out because she gave him away.

After that day, she could not bear the pain, so she just stayed away, however she always wanted her son back. Now she has two other sons, Christian and Nazir, and two daughters, Latoya, and Brielle.

She asked Jackson if they could walk back and see the Daniels to discuss the issue Jackson said, "Ok, that's a start." Jackson rang the doorbell.

Audrey Daniel opened the door, "Hi, Jackson," she said. "Who is this with you?"

Millicent answered and said, "Good day, madam. Is your husband home? Can we please talk? I am Jackson's biological mother, and there are issues which needs to be resolve, Jackson needs to know the truth of his existence."

Audrey Daniel invited her in, offered her a seat, and asked her what can she offer her as to water or juice she accepted water.

There was so much tension.

Pastor Daniel came from his study, and Millicent greeted him, thy introduced themselves.

Millicent said, "First, I would like to apologize. I really would like to express regrets for all the wrong done to such nice people as you, and to Jackson, who is the recipient of all this madness which he did not create or even have any knowledge of.

I am so sorry of this reward to you people for all your good efforts and kindness toward Jackson, but there is one thing I do pray and ask for, and that is for Jackson Simmons, Jackson's biological father, to never get access to him he might ruin him. I have known him enough to know what he can do, and that is no good whatsoever. Jackson is his biological father all right, but for sixteen years of his life, where has he been? You two are the only people he knows."

"Then Jackson said to her, "For sixteen years of my life, where have you been? At least he was in prison, and as soon as he gets out, he went in search of you, wanting to find and get back his son. But as for you, you have not been dead or locked up. Did you come to see me or even care that you had a son"? Explain that. He was so angry."

Jackson said he did not think anyone could understand this sudden shock of finding out that the family you have known all your life suddenly turns fake. "The ones you thought were your blood Where does anyone go from here? Please someone explain to me.

But first allow me a moment to say sorry to the two people who showed kindness and cared for me no matter the problems and trouble I came with. Yet, they still loved and accepted me, not once even having the courage to tell me I had being adopted, not even out of anger, which I am sure I have made them angry countless times.

Chapter Nine

So can you do us all a favor. Just leave and never return. We do not need any apologies from you.

And please, warn that ex-convict that you reference to as my biological father tell him to stay away from this family.

Inform him for me, that if his blood truly runs through my veins, then he should know that I, too, can do crazy things.

And for the record, tell him that I am known as Jack the little Devil in my past life as he is Jack the Reckless Gambler weather in his past or present life. So, one devil should understand and know another devil. So, try me. Tell him not to push me."

Then Jackson got up and left. His biological mother Millicent was in shock. She had de-ja-vu. Is he his father's carbon copy? This reminded her of all the abuse she took from Jackson Simmons, even while pregnant with their child.

And for the first time, the Daniels were immensely proud of their adopted son Jackson stand-up behavior. They thought the name "Jack the little Devil" was fitting, but now they knew why. He was the rightful son of a man also called Jack, the reckless gambler, a crazy tyrant, or more like legions.

After Jackson had walked away, they talked for a while, exchanged information, and said goodnight, leaving everything to the future.

No matter what happens, the Daniels would trust in God and live by faith, not only by sight.

Chapter Ten

Three months went by, before a letter came to the Daniel's home containing a summon telling the Daniels to appear in court to answer the claim from Mister Jackson Simmons, who filled a petition appealing to the authority regarding a particular case involving the adoption of his biological son without his written or his verbal consent.

So, he wanted the court to revoke their former decision in granting legal custody of his son to the Daniel's.

When Jackson Daniel heard of this, he was so furious that he called Millicent his biological mother asking her to come over to see about this, thinking that she might be able to counter sue and prevent Jackson Simmons from succeeding.

In court, Jackson Simmons was triumphant. The courts ruled in his favor, considering that he did not give any kind of consent in anyone adopting his son while he was imprisoned. That was a jubilee for Jackson Simmons, aka Jack the Reckless Gambler, who shouted out his victory in court, saying "No one gambles with me and come out the winner. I was, and still is, Jack the Reckless Gambler. Losers!" he shouted. "Losers!"

Unfortunately for Jackson, he must go live with his biological father, Jackson Simmons.

Only did young Jackson not know living with his biological father Jackson Simmons would be like living in hell with the Devil reincarnated.

All the way home, the Daniels did not speak a word. They did not want to say anything that might trigger off young Jackson.

Ms. Daniel just put on calm gospel songs in place of speaking, hoping that the songs would soothe everyone in the car. Pastor Daniel knew that his wife was applying wisdom to this tough situation.

Meanwhile, he just prayed silently and pondered all this in his heart, knowing that God always made a way and can turn evil into good, finally aloud, he said, "Have Your way, dear Lord."

Jackson was snoring, upon reaching home, they left Jackson in the car with the windows down to continue sleeping, knowing how disappointed he was.

The phone rang. It was Tatiana who called to check up on what transpired in court. Pastor Daniel was in no mood for conversation.

Audrey answered the phone, she, said to Tatiana, "It did not go well. Jackson, unfortunately, must have to go and live with his biological father."

At that moment, Jackson walked into the room and heard the conversation, he replied, "Like hell, I will not. No one can make me go, no one, and someone better tell that fool to stay the hell away from me."

Pastor Daniel came out of his study and said, "Son, calm down. God always has a plan. Just trust in Him. You have lived with me long enough to identify with that. Have faith, my son. Hold fast, this will always be your home, and we will always be your parents even in death.

I will be your father, you can count on that, and as for your mother and four sisters, they will always be your family.

And please, son, as the words of God command "honor thy mother and thy father" with promise, that your days may be long upon the earth. God bless you, my son.

Can you please call up your sister, Nina, Danijela and Hadriana, the twins, while your mom gets Breanna dressed? Let us go and celebrate a family night out together. United we stand, divided we fall. This too shall pass away. No condition remains the same forever.

Audrey Daniel, who was still on the phone with Tatiana, said, "Why not invite Tatiana and her family to join us?"

Chapter Ten

Pastor Daniel said, "That is a great idea, we should invite Jack the reckless gambler. Let us make a formal and friendly request to him."

"More like legions," young Jackson replied. "I never want to see that crazy man again."

Tatiana accepted the invitation she said, "Surely, we would not miss this for the world."

Pastor Daniel hugged his adopted son Jackson and told him to put on his best outfit and look as sharp as a Daniel can, and show him the outfit he chooses, in that case he can try to match up with him." They laughed.

Pastor Daniel's said, "It's called turning an unpleasant situation into something pleasant."

Chapter Eleven

Weeks went by and no words from Jackson Simmons, only a letter from the court allowing the Daniels weekend supervised visit with Jackson, giving time for transition in favor of young Jackson having time to-adjust.

Sixteen years was a lifetime for Jackson, having the Daniels as the only parents and family he knew, so removing him from their home suddenly might result in a dramatic change, this was a tough situation and could cause trauma to young Jackson, hopefully, in time, he might become adjusted to his biological father Jackson Simmons stated the court papers.

However, after all that racket and commotion at the Daniels' home and in family court for his son it had been three months and not a word from Jackson Simmons.

Until today. An old, beaten-up truck rolled up to the Daniels' front yard with music blasting and Jackson Simmons/aka jack the reckless gambler, drunk as a skunk, shouting, and cursing all the curse words known.

"Jackson, my boy! Come on out to your real daddy. Come on, son, let us go live the good life. Your real daddy is going to show them who is the boss," burp, burp. He went staggering as if about to fall flat on his face.

He left the engine running. It was making so much noise, it had no license plate neither front nor back, he then went into all his pockets, emptying them, throwing piles of money to the ground. "All for you, Jackson. My boy, come to your daddy," burp. "I love my boy," coughing from smoking cigarettes.

Pastor Daniel and his wife were out of town, so the neighbor called the police, Jackson Simmons had to get inside the police car, but not before a big struggle, considering how drunk he seemed and the truck he drove was unfit for the road.

Another week passed, and here came the hot head Jackson Simmons, only this time, his son came outside to face his demon of a biological father.

The good news was that, wisely ahead of time, Pastor Daniel his adopted father had coached Jackson Daniel well and prepared him just in case this day would come.

Telling him that by law, when he reached the age of eighteen, he could make his own decisions and very soon, he would be eighteen.

They would keep on praying for him that very soon, all this would pass. And soon they would have a weekend visit. Jackson said, "Ok, Dad. I will try to understand, and I will get to be in church on the weekend visits."

This time Jackson Simmons came with a red sports car; he was sober clean and assertive.

He said, "Hop in, Jackson, my boy." He tried taking Jack's travel bag from him, but Jack pulled away.

The Pastor and his wife stood at the door, looking on at Jackson Simmons as he waved to them and shouted, "I got back my boy, so preacher man, go and adopt a polar bear. Loser!" he shouted as he sped off fast as a race car driver.

Pastor Daniel saw and heard all of that, but he just went back inside and knelt to pray and ask God to keep them both safe, while his wife could not bear to watch her son of sixteen years go off just like that with that lesion of a man who said he fathered Jackson. This was very unbearable for her.

Pastor Titus was right all along. He had told her from the start to not get her hopes too high, just in case disappointment should come from appointment, she just kept on crying.

Chapter Eleven

She only stopped when Jackson walked into the house that weekend. It was joy unspeakable. The girls were all over him, hugging and kissing, laughing, screaming and so chatty.

They all knelt and prayed as per young Jackson knowing that his parents, especially his pastor dad, would really appreciate that gesture.

After church, they all went to a restaurant, and Jack made them laugh so much, as he kept quoting Jackson Simmons his biological father saying, "Come here, Jackson. My boy, come to your real daddy."

"That surely is one statement we are never going to forget to repeat to you, Jackson, my boy," said Pastor Titus Daniel jokingly.

They all cracked up. "This is funny," said little Breanna, the youngest of the girls. She said, "Do tell, Jackson, my boy, how does it feel to have two fathers even if one is a psycho?"

Jackson said, "Don't forget that your brother was a little devil."

"Please, don't remind us," they uttered, laughing, all so delighted in seeing Jackson.

Jackson said that they were staying in a hotel with casinos, a bar and ladies that dressed like bunny's but kind a half-naked. Jackson Simmons his biological father brought two of those ladies to his room and told him that he wanted him to relax and allow them to make him happy.

However, fortunately for him police officers came and arrested Jackson Simmons for a stolen red sport car, Jackson said that Jackson Simmons told the police that he is eighteen, and told him not to worry, because soon he would be back. Jackson said it was only last night that it happened, and it was time for his weekend visit. The ladies left, and so he got his stuff, called a taxi, and came straight home.

Jackson stayed home the next day at the Daniels' home. His adopted parents would not take any chance in allowing him to go back to that hotel where his biological father used as a home for them both "Not possible, not while we are alive," they said. Jackson was all in agreement with that decision.

After four days, the phone rang it was a social worker calling to say that Jackson Simmons called to say that his son was "kidnapped by you people."

Pastor Daniel replied, "I am not in any mood for any more of that man's silly pranks. He has no shame. He is obnoxious and disrespectful, not to mention overbearing and a bold faced, pathological liar, case closed no further discussion."

His wife Audrey said she too had had enough of that crazy man. No more will he disturb their peaceable home. It was enough he had suddenly showed up to claim Jackson without any regard for the two people who carried the burden of raising the boy he now has placed total claim on.

"Not once has he even bothered to greet or even said thanks to us for looking after Jackson."

"He can go to blazes for all I care," said Jackson Daniel, but Pastor Daniel told him to leave the wording to him, as angels are taking down notes of all that we say and do.

"And as a matter of a fact, let us all say a prayer. Lord God, we humbly come to You with this issue. Again, we ask You to watch over Jackson and his father Jackson Simmons.

The child You placed into our care has been a trying of faith and a test, but Lord, I trust you immensely, and I know that all things work for the greater good with you in control.

So, who or what am I to question or even try to wrestle with You? Please, Lord, just keep and see us through this, and may all the honor and glory be unto your name. Thank You in advance, dear Lord, and all said amen."

There was a noise outside. Jackson Simmons came with police officers, and like a mad dog, he jumped out of the police officer's car shouting out, "Kidnappers! Son snatchers! Losers! Where is my son? Jackson, my boy, your daddy his here. Come to your daddy, your real father.

Chapter Eleven

And your name is not anything but Jackson Simmons. You my boy, my mother—— boy No one going to ever steal my boy away from me again, not in this life, not ever, and you can tell that their fake ass pastor boy that I is not no fool, I got brain, I got smartness right up here," he pointed to his head, vomiting up all kind of bad grammar.

The police officers laughed and told him to calm down. They rang the doorbell. Pastor Daniel came to the door he greeted the police officers and ask if he can assist them.

They told him all Jackson Simmons had said at the station and that he wanted to press charges for the kidnapping of his son.

Pastor Daniel explained, and he asked them to allow him to get the visitation rights papers from the court. He then invited them inside because the man was ranting and raging, making so much commotion that it was hard to explain anything in such racket. Pastor Daniel introduced his adopted son Jackson and told him to tell the officers in his own words exactly what he told them transpired that night where he stays with his biological father, Jackson Simmons, right before he came home for his weekend visit.

Jackson did just that, then he told the officers that he did not want to ever go back to that place where is biological father Jackson Simmons called home.

The officers said that they understood, but he had to do as the court orders and advised that Mr. Daniel would have to go and file another petition explaining why he thinks that Jack Simmons is an unfit person to be guardian to his son Jackson and see how it goes.

However as of now, Jackson, cannot be at this house other than what the courts orders. They had to calm Jackson down. He almost jumped out the window, saying he would rather be dead than go back living with that horrifying man.

Meanwhile, Jack the Reckless Gambler was outside puffing cigarettes one after the other and echoing for "Jackson, my boy." The police officers took a report and managed to calmly escort young

Jackson outside. They waited until older Jackson called a cab and left with Jackson, his boy.

"Don't try to play me," he said, shouting, "Fake pastor, bloody kidnappers!"

Pastor closed the door behind him, not saying a word. He just asked his wife for a glass of water, which he sat on his recliner and sipped and stared upward.

Audrey Daniel took out a Bible and read the twenty third Psalms: "The Lord is my Shepherd," and she just sat at her husband's feet, took off his shoes, and massaged them. He looked at her, kissed her forehead, and thanked God for her and their family.

The school bus brought home the youngest girl as the second ones were on campus doing their final year. The oldest was now married and had a family a set of twins a boy, and two girl Samia and Amirah, Christian and Halie were the twin boy's names.

Chapter Twelve

The sermon was a hot topic at church.

Was the sermon about the prodigal son Jackson Daniel? This made everyone in church that day recognize that the pastor was preaching a sermon on faith, hoping that one day, his adopted son Jackson would return to him. It was an incredibly sad day.

At the end of the service, members of the congregation stayed back to show support to the pastor and his family, some said, "God is able," some said, "God has a plan."

After that last weekend visit at the Daniels' home, Jackson Daniel hardly came back, and the few times he came, he did not stay over not even for church, He even shone prayers, he was acting strange, cold, and withdrawn. One could assume that he was changing.

However, that would be an understatement, assuming the influence he has lately.

Pastor Daniel and his wife Audrey fasted and prayed to a point where they lost so much weight and sleep had gone from their eyes. School was on spring break, and the girls were home.

There was no way for them, to disguise the way they looked but was sure that the girls knew the reason

Six months had passed, and they had not heard from or seen their adopted son Jackson, but still yet, in God, they put their trust, and they were waiting on His time, hoping that, for everyone, things would turn out right, even for Jackson Simmons. "Lord, please help him to know You and find his way. Lord, he is Jacksons biological father, so please help him to change and understand and see clearly, Amen."

Finally, they decided to contact Millicent, Jackson's biological mother, who was glad that they did, as she was anxious to know how things were with Jackson, her son, and even Jackson Simmons, but she wanted to avoid that psycho, Jackson Simmons. The Daniels invited her over and updated her on all that had transpired.

She was so sorry but not surprised as to the behavior of (wacko jack the reckless gambler) That was her choice name for him. She even asked if he used his signature line, "Jackson, my boy." She said that while he was around at the beginning of her pregnancy, wacko would talk to her stomach saying, "Jackson, my boy, this your daddy. Are you ok inside, son? Is the light turned on in there?" And then the baby would move as if it understood.

"No joke?" they asked.

"Seriously, no joke," she replied smiling.

She took the phone number and the address of the social worker and promised to stay in touch, informing them on anything she might find out.

The Daniels thanked her and told her to be careful, they could not approach it as there was an order of protection taken out, avoiding Jackson Simmons having any contact with them or them with him.

The only contact was with younger Jackson, their adopted son, and with supervision as per Jackson Simmons's request to the court, now there was none from their adopted son Jackson.

She promised to bring her family to visit, as she wanted them to meet Jackson, their older brother. "let's just keep hope alive," she said Jackson might have a chance of mind. She promised to visit the church. The Daniels told her to be safe and Gods richest blessings on her and her family. She said, "Thanks, and the same to you and your."

Chapter Thirteen

Millicent called the Daniels to tell them an encounter she had with Jackson Simmons and Jackson Daniel their adopted son while on duty at the hospital.

Someone came into the emergency room on a gurney. I recognized it was Jackson Simmons, he was yelling at the top of his lungs saying, "no one messes with me or my boy, and gets away with it, do you know who I am? I am known as Jack the Reckless Gamble" He had a bloodshot eye, and swollen lips.

Please, God, do not let him see me," but as I turned to walk away, who came walking toward me? None other than Jackson, my son.

"Can I get away from this, I thought to myself' my heart pounded, however I managed to say "Hi" to Jackson, who walked past me and went to his father.

I was so amazed by the bond that I saw between them both. When Wacko saw Jackson, they hugged, and Wacko said to Jackson, "You ok, son?"

Jack said, "Yes, Dad. Are you ok?" Wacko then said, "These stupid lazy fools need to get me a cold beer and a cigarette."

To my surprise, right before my eyes, Jackson Daniels pulled out a package of cigarettes and gave one to his dad and then put one in his mouth, got out a lighter, and was about to light up.

I knew that smoking was not permitted in the emergency area, so I approached him and said "no smoking is allowed in this area" Oh boy! Was it my voice or was it my presence?

Jackson Simmons saw that it was me, and he shouted out, "Well I will be darn, if it is not little miss Florence in Nightingale. Where in hell did you come from? Did the cat drag you inside this here smelly fish shop?"

And if that was not bad enough for me, he said to Jackson, "Look, son, it is your runaway train of a mama. So, are you little miss nurse now? Run along, make yourself useful, and get me a six pack of ale I be thirsty."

However, because I was at my job site, I just politely said, "Hello, sir. Are you ok? How can I help you? Are you registered? If not, you cannot see a doctor.

So, your son can take your identification and get you registered. "As soon as Jackson went to do so, I went through another door and caught up with him. Again, I said, "Hi, Jackson." no answer.

However, I continued by asking him, "How are your parents doing? Have you seen them lately?" Still no answer. I went on to say, "I paid them a visit to see how you were doing, but I was surprised when they told me that it has being quite a while, they have not heard from or even set eyes on you. Jackson, that is not fair. They do not deserve this from you they are so broken hearted."

That is when he spoke. And said, "Life is not fair, for so long he has been living a fake life, thinking you both were his real parents, serves you both right for been such devilish saints.

At least now he knows who he really is, Jack the Devil, with a father that he can identify with, Jack the Psycho, according to widely held belief. now he realizes Jackson Simmons is no fake, and he speaks truth and showed him what real life is."

I pleaded. "Jackson," I said. "That is no real life. That kind of life will end you up in jail, if not dead. It is reckless" he replied. "I started this mess, I should end it, get a gun, and shoot them both, go ahead finish it.

He said that I brought Jackson Simmons right back to where he was, in his safe zone, just as his life was turning around for the better. Admit it he said. So do him a favor, go home to my little perfect family.

Chapter Thirteen

I did not drop any of them off in a basket at a church door with a note. So just make like the wind, and blow away, and stay off his case.

Dad!" he shouted. Wacko heard him, and he jumped off the gurney and came hopping to Jackson, his boy.

"This is what I came to tell you people, Millicent said to the Daniel's, "unfortunately I know that it is hard but try your best to go on with your lives. Look out for your girls and allow those two to work out their situation, let us just keep praying that God will arrest them and keep them in His arms of love. Bye for now, I will call you or come by to see you all from time to time."

Chapter Fourteen

Audrey Daniels ran to the bathroom to throw up, she had done this quite a couple of time, her husband suggested that she see the family doctor. Who ran tests, and the results showed that she was eight weeks pregnant.

Months later, Audrey Daniel, after a very painful delivery, gave birth to twins for the second time only this time the universe had favored them and gave them twin boys; to God be the glory.

Still yet, they did not forget about their adopted son Jackson Daniel.

Each time the family prayed, they included Jackson their adopted son and his biological parents.

Millicent frequently attended Pastor Daniel's church together with her husband Mark Hines and their four children.

Tatiana was a key player in the Daniel's life, especially now that the family had extended, they even hired two ladies, Ms. Olga, and Ms. Lola, to help with the twin boys.

A year passed, and no prodigal son had returned. Instead, it all over the news: "Wanted for questioning: two males, an adult, and a boy of around seventeen years old broke into and robbed a liquor, and a grocery store; the suspects have remarkable resemblance, they could be father and son, or even brothers. If seen, do not approach them, they could be armed and dangerous contact the police.

Jackson Simmons was cunning and notorious. Each time a crime was committed, and their identities exposed, he would change locations, taking Jackson, his boy with him.

"Wanted" posters were everywhere possible.

Young Jackson Daniel was living his new life with his biological and troubled father Jackson Simmons, and he was enjoying every moment of it.

This wild and dangerous lifestyle was sweet to young Jackson Daniel. Prostitutes, liquor, drugs gambling, fast cars, and loads of money stolen from anywhere possible or gained from gambling.

Young Jackson once even quoted a Bible scripture to his dad as a joke after committing an armed robbery in a parking lot, robbing an elderly man's wallet.

He quoted by saying the Bible says, "One can seek bread in desolate places," and added in "desperate times." They giggled after putting the elderly man to sit on the floor of a parking lot. The elderly man told the police that it was two scallywags that robbed him. They wore scarves over their faces as means of disguise. They got in a car and Jackson Simmons was driving way past the speed limit, which is when the police indicated to the driver to stop, however the driver stepped on the accelerator and drove even faster. And made it to the place where they stayed.

Cops give chase; and called for backup, helicopters were flying over the hotel after someone reported that two men ran from a car inside the hotel. They tried to escape, the police caught and arrested them.

The police found a gun on Jackson Simmons who subsequently told the arresting police officers that young Jackson, was not a part of any crime, plus he was underage, so young Jackson walked, while the older Jackson picked up the charges for theft and armed robbery, tried and sentenced to nine months in prison and one year probation.

Young Jackson often visited Jackson Simmons in the prison who coached and steered him from there.

He told Jackson to take care of himself from the money stolen and, from what they won in casinos gambling. Young Jackson Daniel even mentioned to his biological father Jackson Simmons that he wanted to change his name from Daniel to Simmons, which pleased his father very much.

Chapter Fifteen

Then something happened one evening, Jackson ran into his eldest adopted sister Nina, they both froze at seeing each other. She first made a move toward Jack and hugged him, suddenly a man came out of a car grabbed her, then hit and called her names.

He was about to approach young Jackson, who pulled out a gun and fired a shot at the man. His sister run toward them, as to try and stop them and to tell Jack that the man was her jealous husband, Javien.

It was already too late. Unfortunately for her the bullet from Jack's gun took its mark, and pierced through her left shoulder.

She blamed her husband for causing the incident, but she told Jackson, "Sorry," and it was not his fault, she asked him to leave the scene in case the police came, and he might get arrested, her husband had taken off when Jackson fired the shot.

Jack stopped a cab, got in with her, and made sure she got to the hospital for treatment before he left.

And for the period of six months, while his biological father Jackson Simmons was in prison young Jackson live lavishly, spending and blowing money like a rich person.

Worse thing was that Jackson Simmons's old time crime partner name Curly Joe was discharged from prison.

Young Jackson ended up staying with his father's crime partner, Curly Joe as a request from Jackson Simmons Jackson's biological father.

Once again, Jackson had an even worse influence. He partied with his father's friend sons Earl, Trevor and Leroy, and their friends. They lived in a big mansion with a swimming pool.

One day, they had a pool party and young Jackson had gotten drunk and fell into the pool, if not for Bianca, Brazil and Bo' Jacksons father's friend Curly Joe's daughters, jumping into the pool and rescuing him, he might have drowned.

They had to pump water from Jackson and rush him to the hospital almost unconscious.

Jackson had so much alcohol and drugs in his blood that the doctors said, "If he survives, it will take a miracle."

The saddest thing was that his biological mother, Millicent, was on duty that same day at the hospital when Jackson Daniel came in. She told the doctors, and her nursing collogues that he is her son.

And for three full weeks, Jackson had been on a respirator. The doctors were doing everything to try and save his life.

Millicent called the Daniels to give them the new on what had happened to their adopted son Jackson, it was now time for prayers. Pastor Daniels went to the hospital to be at his adopted son's side. He brought with him a Bible and his prayer shawl. He sat by the bedside of Jackson for two days, reading to him and praying to God for him to wake up and be ok.

Who was it that said, "The effectual fervent prayers of a righteous man avails much" (quote unquote) (James:5, 16.KJV)

Jackson sneezed, opened his eyes, and started removing everything attached to him, He saw his adopted father Pastor Titus Daniel sitting by his bedside, but he just got up and walked past him ignoring him and walked out of the hospital.

Pastor Daniel was just thankful that his adopted son Jackson was back he kneeled and prayed, giving thanks and praises to God Almighty for answering prayers.

When Pastor Titus Daniel got home from the hospital and told his wife all that had happened, how Jackson woke up and saw him but did not even say hello to him, she replied by saying, "That's how a devil usually acts, and don't forget, Jack says that he is a 'little devil.'"

Chapter Fifteen

She smiled and said, "Are you hungry? Have a shower while I get you something to eat, you look terrible." Pastor Daniel was so happy that Jackson was all right.

When Jackson got outside, he jumped into a taxi and went straight to the prison to visit his father, who was quite elated to see his Jackson boy after not seeing or hearing from him for weeks.

He told his biological father Jackson Simmons what had happened to him, at Curly Joe's home his father Jackson Simmons was furious and wanted to strangle his friend Curly Joe.

Who was already so afraid to tell Jackson Simmons what had happened to his son, knowing that if his boy Jackson had drowned in the pool at his home, he would be a dead man when Jack the reckless gambler got out of prison.

Young Jackson had such a terrible headache that he fainted at the prison, and had to be taken to the closest hospital, after examining him the doctor said he needs something to eat.

Chapter Sixteen

Jackson Simmons came out of prison with one year probation left, in which if violated, he would go back. When Jackson Simmons got out of prison, he went straight to his friend Curly Joe's home and beat him up so badly for not informing him that his son almost drowned in his swimming pool.

Curly Joe's sons were not at home, to see when Jack the Reckless Gambler threw their father into the swimming pool. and said, "No one will save your stupid, dumb ass. Go to hell and tell your maker I sent you and inform his fiery ass not to expect him or his boy Jackson down there any time soon."

He then walked away, luckily for Curly Joe he was a very good swimmer, so he made it out from the pool weak and tired but alive.

He fell on the floor and yelled, "Jack, you dirty son of a prostitute!" coughing as he took a breath and back to yelling and cursing at Jack the reckless gambler.

Young Jackson has just rolled up in a cab, and his father said, "Get back into the cab, we are leaving. I just killed that worthless son of an ugly witch," and he spat on the ground and said, "Die, you bastard."

While inside the cab, Jackson Simmons was vomiting all kind of curse words to the driver, telling him to stop driving the car like a darn snail.

He threatened not to pay him one penny in fare since he was going too slow and making him late for work and his son late for school, which had not one iota of the truth to it. He was just trying to intimidate the driver because he had no money to pay the fare. Young Jackson kept quiet, as he knew what his cunning father was up to.

One block before they reached their destination, the older Jackson said to the cab driver sternly, "Pull over and stop this car," he opened the door and got out. Jackson, his boy, also got out. His father slammed the car door shut and kicked the side of the car, stuck up his middle finger at the driver and walked away.

The driver was already praying in his mind for them to get out. He was happy that the crazy passenger did not attack him, he drove off.

Older Jackson rubbed his boy Jacksons head, threw his arms around him, and said to him, "Son, this is called 'survival of the fittest' and the bold ones." "Jackson said, "Dad, I am learning."

His father said, "I love you, son." Jackson Simmons then went over to a tree and peed right in the open and said, "Son, come over here and take a pee up this tree. I am going into that jewelry store. Get ready to run if you must, just stay outside and cover me, we need cash." He came out of the jewelry store bloody but loaded with cash, jewelry, and a gun. He even had the key to the jewelry store, so he locked the door behind him. Grinning from ear to ear, "Jackson, my boy," he said. "Let us go eat and find a place to rest for tonight, tomorrow we can figure out the rest."

He took off his blood-stained shirt and wiped himself clean enough. Lucky enough for him, he had on an under shirt. "This will work just fine," he mumbled.

They got into a cab, went to a restaurant, ate a hardy meal, then to a barber shop and next a pub, they got drunk, bought cigarettes, marijuana and supplies, a bottle of liquor, and then checked into a motel.

Proud Jackson Simmons bragged about how he pulled of his robbery in the jewelry store, as if giving his son lessons on how to survive by any means possible.

He said that he walked into the store, and just one couple was there looking at jewelry. He was looking around at the artwork hanging on the walls of the jewelry story, biding his time, and checking out the store, looking for cameras.

"Then as soon as the couple left, the old guy at the counter asked sir, 'Can I help you?' so I used a kind a foreign accent to answer him, not wanting to waste time, I said, 'I want to help you get rid of some jewelry and money.' The man bent down as if to reach for something.

That is when I made my move. I jumped over the counter, grabbed him, and punched him in his face. That is how he got blood all over me.

Man, it was a struggle. The old guy put up a good fight, so I really let him know who was boss. He fell flat on his face, moaning like a real fool.

That is when I got this sack and loaded it with cash and all kinds of fine jewelry and this baby, he kissed the gun and gave it to Jackson, saying, "Son, this is for protection. This is the only God we need.

This is what we, the bigger boys, call scoring or hitting a home run.

Do not worry yourself, Jackson, my boy. We are going to be years of billions, ah, ah, ah," laughing aloud.

They drank, smoked, counted the money, and separated the jewelry, selecting and sorting by value and weight in order accordingly the value of stolen items.

Jackson Simmons had his buyers, so it was no problem for him to sell. Getting rid of them was a synch. Finally, they fell asleep, and they slept for a full day.

Chapter Seventeen

It was gradation day for the Daniel's twin girls.
Danijela and Hadriana.

After the gradation ended, they went to a restaurant to eat and celebrate the girls' achievement. To everyone's surprise, who walked inside the restaurant but Jackson one and two, like two peas in a pod.

The girls were so happy to see Jackson their long-lost brother that they jumped from their seats and ran to him, hugging him and telling him how much they missed him. They invited him to Come sit with them. Say hi to mom and dad.

Look Jack, your twin brothers? Johnathan and Jeremiah soon. They will be one year old, them too has a cat named, 'Bobcat,' just like the one Dad has bought for you," which got Jackson's attention that he held both their hands and walked over to their table, Jackson said, "Hi, Mom. Hi, Dad." The twin boys were staring at him. Jack picked them both up, one in each arm, and held them hugging them. His adopted parents just sat there, not saying a word.

Jackson Simmons said as he sat down at their table, "Well, well, if you can't beat them, might as well join them." He then pulled a plate of their food over to him and started eating it while mumbling grammars.

Pastor Daniel said, "Go ahead, join us help yourself. "Jackson Simmons said, "What is it with you people? Are you punks or just dumb fools?"

Young Jackson Daniel, answered Jackson Simmons his biological father and said, "Yes, we are, but you are even a bigger punk and the dumbest fool."

Jackson Daniel was now a man and old enough to walk away from his biological father Jackson Simmons and to make his own decisions—not the court, not anyone.

He then sat the twin boys down and walked out of the restaurant. Jackson Simmons aka Jack the reckless gambler got up and went after him.

He grabbed Jackson by his shirt collar and tried to sucker punch him, but younger Jackson, aka Jack the Little Devil, gave a beating to Jackson, aka the Reckless Gambler, one he was not expecting or might not forget anytime soon.

Jackson Daniel then stopped a cab, and by the time the Daniels got home, Jackson was waiting outside. His adopted father Pastor Titus Daniel just said, "Welcome home, Jackson Daniel and gave praise to God, whose time is always the best. "Pastor Daniel said to Jackson son, never give up on God, who will never give up on you."

The prodigal son had returned home. Years passed, and Jackson Daniel was fifth in line to become a pastor in the Daniel's family.

The Bible states, "Train up a child in the way he or she should go and when they are old it will not depart from them."

Jackson Simmons was subsequently caught with the stolen items, convicted, and sentenced to serve time without parole.

The end
P. Dalton Simms

Epilogue

He wrote a letter to Jackson Daniel, his preacher son. These are the contents of the letter.

My dearest son Jackson,

I am writing this letter from my prison cell while having so many regrets. Son, it is ok for you to go ahead and label me as being innocently foolish or even ignorant.

Last night in the prison's recreation hall, I was watching the television, and there was a preacher whose message convicted and got my deepest attention, but son, when I saw that it was you preaching, it got my attention even more I just stood there as if frozen.

Other inmates had to check if I was a goner. Someone called out my name Jackson, and I jumped up, shouting, "That is my boy Jackson Daniel Simmons and that their preacher man is the man that took my boy in and brought him up for sixteen long years while I was wasting my life away in prison! That preacher man is my good friend." But in my heart, I knew I was lying. But everyone already knows that I am professionally everything sinful and bad, so they just humored me.

Son, I am so proud of you, and I am proud to be your biological father, but your adopted father Pastor Daniel, Jackson my son, you got my sincere permission from today to call him "father," and as for his wife, please give her my highest regards. Tell her I will be home soon because I am sure that you all are praying for my release.

And if you happen to see your mamma Millicent, please tell her I would really appreciate it, if she would come to visit me in this here hell-hole prison so that I can personally tell her "Sorry" to her face. I will even kneel and ask her forgiveness.

I am the father of one male child, but as of now, I am the father of all children, Jackson my son, soon as I come out of this prison, I am coming to that church, and the pastor man and you can dip me in the pool seven times.

I might even need far more dipping than that, but we will leave it for the bigger man up there to do, Jackson my preacher son, you are now a grown man, please take my advice be good crime pays dearly in the worst possible ways .

Forever in my heart, Jackson Daniel Simmons peace and love,

    Your daddy Jackson Simmons, the changed man.

www.ingramcontent.com/pod-product-compliance
Ingram Content Group UK Ltd.
Pitfield, Milton Keynes, MK11 3LW, UK
UKHW041956230426

12048UKWH00008B/371